Little Ogre's Surprise Supper

D0981449

About the author and illustrator:

Timothy Knapman has written lots of picture books as well as plays and musicals. Timothy lives in Surrey in the UK – and firmly believes that it is okay to play with your food!

Ben Cort is the bestselling, award-winning illustrator of over eighty books for children – and he's written one too. Just like Jack, Ben would love to have supper with Little Ogre as he loves vegetable stew too!

To Louis, Millie and Felix, good enough to eat, with love – T.K.

With all my love to my two little ogres,
Johnny and Anna! – B.C.

First published 2010 by Macmillan Children's Books
This edition published 2014 by Macmillan Children's Books
a division of Macmillan Publishers Limited
20 New Wharf Road, London N1 9RR
Basingstoke and Oxford
Associated companies throughout the world
www.panmacmillan.com

ISBN: 978-1-4472-4531-5

Text copyright © Timothy Knapman 2010
Illustrations copyright © Ben Cort 2010
Moral rights asserted

2 4 6 8 9 7 5 3 1

A CIP catalogue record for this book is available from the British Library.

Printed in China

Little Ogre's Surprise Supper

Timothy Knapman

Illustrated by Ben Cort

MACMILLAN CHILDREN'S BOOKS

This is my mum. She's beautiful, isn't she?
And tomorrow is her birthday.

She's going to be 103!

I spent yesterday decorating our cave and getting
everything ready for the party. But I'm also going to
cook her a surprise supper as a special birthday treat.
The problem is that Mum is a fussy eater.

"I don't eat kings," she says, "they're too rich."
"I don't eat princesses," she says, "they're too sweet."
"I don't eat knights," she says, "I don't like
tinned food."

And the only time she ever ate a wizard — in a fancy restaurant up in town — it did extremely peculiar things to her tummy.

So I was glad to find Jack. Look at him:
he's fresh, there's plenty of good meat on
him and he smells delicious.

"I want to have you for supper," I said.
But then Jack did a funny thing.

He didn't scream. He didn't run away. He didn't try to hide. He said, "Thank you! No one's ever had me to supper before." And he gave me a **big** hug.

I think he may have misunderstood me. He was certainly very cheerful all the way home.

And we had such fun at the party! Jack was brilliant at pass the castle and pin the tail on the dragon.

Usually Mum doesn't like me playing with my food, but this time I couldn't stop myself. I took Jack up to my room and showed him all my toys.

Then we went into the garden to feed my pets.
They liked Jack so much they rolled over and
he tickled their tummies.

(No one's ever done that before!)

Soon it was time to get supper ready.
Somehow I wasn't looking forward to
it as much as I'd been expecting.

"Don't worry," said Jack. "It must be boring
washing vegetables on your own. I'll help you."
So we washed them together.
"Is there something the matter?" he asked.

I must say, Jack did look a bit surprised when I put him into the cooking pot.

"I always wash my hands before supper," he said. "But I don't usually have a bath as well. You ogres must be very clean!"

As I was sharpening the knife, I thought it was about time I explained something to Jack.

But before I could get the chance he said,
"You know, there aren't any other children
where I live, so I don't get to play with anyone
very often. Today has been the best day ever!"

And that made me think of all the
times I've asked people if they'd
like to play with me.

They usually scream . . .

and run away . . .

. . . and try to hide.

It's a funny thing, chopping onions always makes me cry.

But there are times when you have to do things that are very difficult. This was one of those times. So I got on with cooking supper.

And that day (you're going to hate me for this),
that day I cooked (but really, I didn't have any choice)

That day I cooked my mum a supper.
(I mean, what would you have done?)
That day I cooked my mum a supper of . . .

. . . vegetable stew. SURPRISE!

Mum said it was the best meal she'd ever eaten and
I had to agree. After all, it's not every day you have
your best friend for supper!